Johanna Hurwitz

BUSYBODY NORA

Illustrated by Lillian Hoban

MORROW JUNIOR BOOKS / NEW YORK

Printed in the United States of America.
1 2 3 4 5 6 7 8 9 10

Library of Congress Cataloging-in-Publication Data
Hurwitz, Johanna.
Busybody Nora / by Johanna Hurwitz: illustrated by Lillian Hoban.
p. cm.
Summary: Relates the adventures of an inquisitive little girl who
lives in a large apartment building in New York with her parents and
little brother Teddy.
ISBN 0-688-09092-3.—ISBN 0-688-09093-1 (lib. bdg.)
[1. Apartment houses—Fiction. 2. City and town life—Fiction.]
I. Hoban, Lillian, ill. II. Title.
PZ7.H9574Bu 1990 89-13649
[E]—dc20 CIP
AC

Contents

For Nomi and Beni and the real Mrs. W.

Mrs. Mind-Your-Own-Business and the Other Neighbors

Two hundred people lived in the same house with Nora and her brother Teddy.

Their home was an apartment building in New York City. The building had eight floors, and there were five apartments on each floor. Some apartment buildings are much, much larger, but this one was large enough.

Nobody had ever counted all the people, but

Nora had once told her mother, "A million people live in our building."

Mommy had corrected her. "Not a million, but maybe two hundred," she said. That number was big enough; it fascinated Nora and stuck in her head.

She liked to imagine the other people in the building. It was funny to think about 199 other people all brushing their teeth at the same time. Or 199 other people all putting slices of bread in their toasters. Or 199 other people turning out the light to go to sleep.

Yet even though they lived in the same building, and she had been there all her life, which was five years going on six, Nora hadn't seen all the people. She knew all the dog owners because they often rode in the elevator with their pets and took these pets for walks along the street in front of the house. Nora and Teddy counted seven different dogs in their building: two dachshunds, a poodle, a German shepherd, and three mutts. Their favorite dog was a mutt named Putzi, who could carry

a small bag of groceries in her mouth for her owner. Nora and Teddy knew the names of all of the dogs and greeted them whenever they saw them. Someday they hoped they would have a dog too.

"Or how about an alligator?" asked Teddy.

"An alligator!" Mommy gasped, the first time he suggested it. "Where would we put an alligator?"

"In the bathtub, of course," answered Teddy.

"If we had an alligator," said Mommy, "we probably wouldn't have very many friends."

They had some very special friends who lived in the building. There was Mrs. Wurmbrand, who had lived in the building since before Mommy and Daddy were born. Now Mrs. Wurmbrand was over eighty years old. She often came in the evening to have coffee and to visit with Mommy. She always brought chocolates for Nora and Teddy. She was like an extra grandmother, even more real than their other grandmothers, because she had white hair and she looked old the way grandmothers always looked in books. They called her

Mrs. W. for short. Once, when he was little, Teddy asked Mommy if there was a Mrs. A. and a Mrs. B. and a Mrs. C. There wasn't even a Mr. W. He had died many years before. But Mrs. W., whose grown children lived in a faraway city, said that she considered Nora and Teddy and their parents to be her family too.

Once an apartment became vacant. Nora hoped more children would move into it. But instead the new neighbors were a man and a woman with no children. Not even a dog.

Luckily they still had their friend Russell, who was only two and who lived on the second floor.

"Maybe when he is three, he will move to the third floor," said Teddy.

Russell was eleven months younger than Teddy, so for one month both boys were the same age. But then Teddy got ahead again. Russell was too little to care, anyhow. Teddy, though, liked being a year older and could not understand why for a whole month he had been the same age as little Russell.

What bothered Nora was that she didn't know

the names of *all* the people. Henry, the doorman, whose job it was to stand in the lobby and open the door for the tenants, knew everybody's name. Nora listened with amazement when she heard him.

"How did you learn all the names?" she once asked him.

"It's from seeing the same faces over and over again," Henry explained. "I've seen you every day since you were born practically, so it would be pretty hard to forget your name."

"I guess you know me as well as my mommy and daddy," said Nora.

"Me too," said Teddy.

"How can I learn everyone's name?" Nora asked her mother.

"You'll just have to ask them, I suppose," answered Mommy.

And to her mother's surprise and also to the surprise of all their neighbors, that is exactly what Nora did.

Whenever they got into the elevator to ride up or down from their seventh-floor apartment and another person was present, Nora would ask, "What is your name?"

Some people would smile and tell their name and ask Nora what her name was too. Others would pretend to ignore her and her question. One cross woman, carrying a heavy bag of groceries, just glared at Nora and said, "Mrs. Mind-Your-Own-Business."

Nora looked at the woman with astonishment. "Is that really your name?" she asked.

"Hush!" Mommy said to Nora.

Just then the grocery bag tore, and cans of soup and juice spilled onto the elevator floor. Nora quickly bent to help pick up the food. Her head bumped into the bent head of Mrs. Mind-Your-Own-Business, so instead of saying "Thank you," the woman said "Ouch!" And then she muttered, "You little busybody!"

The elevator stopped at their floor, and Mommy pulled Nora by the hand before she could say

anything more. Afterward Nora always called the woman by that whole long name, Mrs. Mind-Your-Own-Business, but not to her face, of course.

Some days Mommy said she found it too embarrassing to ride in the elevator down from the seventh floor with Nora acting like a special investigator from the FBI.

"Who is that?" asked Nora. "What apartment does he live in?"

For many weeks, Nora asked people their names. Some of the names she learned were those of delivery men, a postman named Tom with a registered letter, and an insurance salesman. Others were relatives and friends of the other tenants. Some of the names she forgot, like that of the insurance salesman, but most of the names she remembered. She knew Mrs. Gross, who lived on the fifth floor, and Mr. and Mrs. De Negris, who lived on the eighth floor. And she became friendly with a woman named Anita, who lived on the seventh floor, across the hall from them.

"Do you know what?" Nora asked Henry. "Since

we all live together in the same house, we should all do special things together."

"What do you have in mind?" he asked her.

"Well, we could have a great big party for everyone," suggested Nora. "Two hundred people blowing out candles, two hundred people eating ice cream, two hundred people singing together. I'll ask my mother if we could have a giant party."

"I doubt it," said Henry. "In fact, I would say never."

"Maybe," said Mommy, which was the way she sometimes said no.

"I think, Nora," she said, "you had better plan your entertaining on a smaller scale."

"How do you weigh it?" asked Teddy.

Stone Soup for Supper

Tuesday night there were spaghetti and meatballs for supper. Daddy was out of town on a business trip, and so as a treat Mommy made the children's favorite meal. Nora ate two portions, and Teddy ate three. They both had red beards and moustaches and full stomachs when they finished.

On Wednesday Teddy announced, "Tonight I want you to cook *my* favorite food."

15

"I thought *spaghetti* was your favorite," said Mommy.

"Not anymore. It's Nora's favorite, not mine. Tonight I want *mine*," demanded Teddy.

"OK," agreed Mommy. She thought Teddy would ask for hot dogs or French toast. But he surprised her.

"I want stone soup."

"Stone soup! That's just a story," Mommy said, laughing. "The three soldiers only pretend that they can make soup from a stone to trick the people into sharing their food. Everyone gives something for seasoning, and soon there's a big pot of soup. Don't you remember? I can't really make it. Besides, how do you know it's your favorite? You don't eat any vegetables. Stone soup has lots of vegetables."

"I love vegetables in stone soup," said Teddy.

"Well, we don't even have any stones," explained Mommy. "Besides, it's raining outside so we can't go to the park to look for stones."

"We have a stone!" cried Nora. She had been

16

sitting very quietly listening to Teddy's discussion with Mommy. Now she ran to the bedroom. On Daddy's desk was a large, smooth stone picked up on a beach in Maine before she and Teddy were born.

Teddy ran to his bedroom and returned with the library book called *Stone Soup* that Mommy had read at bedtime the night before. "Here is the cookbook," he called out.

"That's not a cookbook," said Mommy, but she opened the book and began mumbling to herself about onions, carrots, potatoes. . . .

"Hurrah!" shouted Nora and Teddy, jumping up and down. "Stone soup for supper."

Mommy went to the refrigerator and took out some carrots. "I think I'm all out of onions," she remembered. "Nora, you can go upstairs and ask Mrs. Wurmbrand if we may borrow an onion. No," she corrected herself, "ask if she could spare two onions."

"I want to go!" shouted Teddy.

"All right, go together," said Mommy. "You can

take this measuring cup and stop at the Michaels'
too. Ask Mrs. Michaels if she has any barley. And
remember, don't ring the doorbell. Just knock
softly. Little Russell may be asleep. It's time for
his afternoon nap." Since Russell was two years
old, he still took naps like a baby.

Nora and Teddy didn't wait for the elevator.
They ran up the flight of stairs to the eighth floor.
They rang Mrs. Wurmbrand's bell and waited for
her slow steps. As they stood there, the apartment
door next to Mrs. W.'s opened. Out walked Mrs.
Mind-Your-Own-Business, wearing a raincoat and
rainhat and carrying an umbrella.

"What are you children doing standing here in
the hall?" she demanded. "Does your mother know
that you are running about?"

"We came to borrow two onions," explained
Nora.

"For stone soup," Teddy added.

"Your mother should plan her shopping better,"
observed Mrs. Mind-Your-Own-Business, as she
got onto the elevator.

"Let's not invite her to have any soup," Nora whispered to Teddy. "But we can invite Mrs. Wurmbrand and Russell, because they are going to lend us food."

The door opened and Mrs. W. greeted her young friends warmly, inviting them inside. "Nora, why aren't you at school today?" asked Mrs. Wurmbrand. The children explained that it was spring recess and that kindergarten was closed all week.

Downstairs Mommy scrubbed the stone that had been sitting as a paperweight on Daddy's desk all these years.

A half hour passed before the children returned. Their mouths showed that Mrs. W. had given them each some chocolate as well as the onions. And they had stopped to try out Russell's new tricycle, which *he* didn't even know how to ride yet.

Mommy cut up the onions and put them in her largest pot, which was already filled with boiling water and the stone. Both children climbed up on chairs to peek inside the pot. Next their mother cut up the carrots.

"Did you remember to put in salt and pepper?" asked Teddy. He had a good memory for a boy his age.

Mommy put in the pepper and the barley.

"I have powdered mashed potatoes, potato chips, and frozen French fries," she told Nora and Teddy. "I don't have any real potatoes. Shall we just leave them out?"

"Oh no!" the children protested. "We can't leave anything out."

"Let's borrow some from Anita," suggested Nora. Anita was their prettiest neighbor. She lived by herself in a tiny apartment, and she had long red fingernails and long blond hair. She was a schoolteacher, home on vacation, just like Nora. So off went the children across the hall to borrow the potatoes.

They returned with potatoes and also a small bag of mushrooms.

"Anita said these were left over from the dinner she cooked last night," Nora explained. "And she showed me how she puts on eyelashes. I'd like

some extra eyelashes for my next birthday. I think they will come in handy."

"Handy for what?" asked Mommy, as she peeled the potatoes.

Teddy looked nervously into the bag of mushrooms. "Are you sure these aren't poison mushrooms?" he demanded. He was remembering the mushrooms in the *Story of Babar,* another of his favorite books.

"I don't know who would have a cabbage," said Mommy. But then she answered herself. "Yes, I do! Mrs. Murphy was in line behind me at the supermarket yesterday. She had a cabbage in her wagon. Go and ask her if she could spare us a few leaves from it, if they haven't already eaten it."

Mrs. Murphy lived on the ground floor, so the children took the elevator. Before long they returned with the cabbage.

It was added to the pot, together with a piece of meat cut off from the pot roast Mommy was going to cook the next night when Daddy came home.

All afternoon the children took turns stirring the pot. The kitchen had a lovely smell. It wasn't carrots or potatoes or meat or barley or cabbage; it was stone soup. When their favorite TV program began, they left the kitchen, but the good smell followed them into the living room.

At six o'clock, as Mommy was just about to serve supper, the doorbell rang.

It was Mr. and Mrs. Michaels with Russell. "It was so nice of you to invite us to have supper with you. I love spur-of-the-moment invitations. They are the most fun!" Mrs. Michaels handed Mommy a package of ice cream. "I had this in the freezer, and I thought I would contribute it to the meal."

As they stood at the open door, the elevator door opened too. Mrs. W. stepped out. She was wearing her best dress. "Aren't you kind to invite a lonely old woman to dinner on such a rainy, gloomy day," she said, handing Mommy a box of imported cookies in a lovely tin.

"We can put our crayons in the box when it's empty," whispered Nora to Teddy.

Mommy looked very surprised. But she was also very polite. "Let's all come inside," she said.

The guests came in, and Mommy rushed to get some more bowls. "I hadn't finished setting the table," she explained.

The doorbell rang. It was Anita with a bottle of wine. "I can't stay long. I have a date in about an hour," she apologized. "Unless Paul would like to stay here."

After Anita came Mr. and Mrs. Murphy. Mrs. Murphy carried a steaming platter of meat. "This was already in the oven when your children came downstairs," explained Mrs. Murphy. "It tastes so much better hot. I hope you won't be offended that I brought it."

Mommy looked at the platter. The meat was surrounded by brown potatoes. Mr. Murphy stood next to his wife holding a pitcher of gravy.

They went into the dining alcove, and they greeted the other guests. Teddy sat on his high stool grinning happily and Nora was handing out paper napkins, when the doorbell rang again.

"Who else is coming?" Mommy whispered to Nora.

"I don't know. We didn't ask anyone else."

Mommy went to the door and opened it.

It was Daddy!

"Surprise!" he said. "I was able to get away from the conference early."

"We have a surprise too," said Nora and Teddy, hugging Daddy.

"For supper we are having *stone soup*!"

"And company," said Mommy.

It was just like the book. "And I will eat all the vegetables," promised Teddy.

"And the ice cream," said Nora.

Nora the Baby-Sitter

Thursdays and Fridays were always fun. Thursday was Mommy's "day off." Mommy went out by herself, and Mrs. Michaels came upstairs with Russell and was the baby-sitter. On Friday, Mrs. Michaels also came upstairs with Russell, only on that day she left him and went out while Mommy was his baby-sitter. The apartment that Nora and Teddy lived in was a large one with more room for

27

running about, which is why Russell came upstairs both days.

"Where are you going today?" asked Nora. She was watching Mommy put on her earrings. They were special "going-out" earrings that hung down, and she noticed that her mother had also put on lipstick.

"I'm going to get a haircut," said Mommy. "And then I'm going to meet my friend Elsa at the Metropolitan Museum for lunch."

Teddy was walking about the room wearing Mommy's good shoes. He watched her getting ready to go out, but he didn't cry. Ever since Mommy and Mrs. Michaels began to exchange baby-sitting he liked it when Mommy went out.

Their mother looked at the clock. "Nora, Mrs. Michaels will be here in five minutes. I have to stop at the bank, and I'm afraid there may be a long line and I'll be late. Will you be a big girl and take care of Teddy? Listen for the doorbell and ask who is it before you open the door."

Nora said yes, proudly. Sometimes Mommy left

her alone for a few minutes, when she went to the laundry room in the basement or to get the mail. It made Nora feel very grown-up, and Mommy said that it taught her responsibility. After all, soon she would finish kindergarten, and then she would be in first grade.

Teddy kissed Mommy good-bye.

Nora kissed Mommy good-bye on the lips, hoping some of the lipstick would come off on her.

Then Nora sat on the sofa and pretend read a book. It was *Madeline,* and she knew every word by heart. Just as she finished, the doorbell rang.

"It's Mrs. Michaels," called Teddy from his bedroom. He was building a block bridge and was afraid to lift his hand for fear that the entire structure would collapse.

"Who is it?" Nora asked from her side of the door.

"Russell and his mommy," called the voice from the other side.

Nora opened the door. There stood Mrs. Michaels. Instead of her usual slacks and ponytail, she was wearing a dress and her hair was pinned up on her head.

"Nora, sweetie, thank your mother for changing days with me. I've got to run. I have a doctor's appointment. See you at three o'clock, Russell," she said, kissing the top of her little boy's head.

And suddenly she was inside the elevator and gone.

Nora closed the door and locked it. "Russell," she said, in a voice full of wonder. "Today I am going to have lots of responsibility."

Russell smiled. He didn't speak yet, but Nora knew that he understood her when she spoke.

He started to run to the children's room, and Nora went after him. She was just in time to keep him from crashing into the bridge.

"This is the George Washington Bridge," said Teddy. "Don't you dare touch it."

"Here, Russell," said Nora, grabbing some unused blocks on the floor. "I'll help you build the Brooklyn Bridge." Diverted, Russell sat on the floor piling up blocks.

When the boys got tired of building, Nora offered to read to them. She pretend read *Madeline* three times and *Curious George* two times. She didn't miss a single word. Teddy would have corrected her if she had, because he also knew the stories by heart.

After reading so much, Nora was thirsty. She went to the refrigerator and took out a container of milk. Then she pushed a chair up close to the cupboard and took down the bottle of chocolate syrup. She made three glasses of chocolate milk, extra chocolaty. The three children drained their glasses.

"You're a good baby-sitter," said Teddy, as he rubbed off his chocolate moustache. "What's for lunch?"

There was a pause, but only for an instant. "Peanut-butter sandwiches."

"That's good," approved Teddy. The children always had peanut-butter sandwiches for lunch, whether it was Mommy or Mrs. Michaels baby-sitting.

Lunch was very good, even though Russell got peanut butter in his hair.

Then they all played house. Teddy was the daddy, and Nora was the mommy. Of course, Russell was the baby. Next they played ball, rolling several balls to each other, all at the same time. And then Nora decided it was time for Russell's nap. But Russell didn't seem at all tired. He kept running about, and he wouldn't lie down on either Teddy's or Nora's bed.

Nora had an idea. "Let's all lie down together on Mommy's and Daddy's big bed."

The three children climbed up on the big bed. First they lay quietly. But then Teddy began to jump and bounce. And then Russell started jumping too.

"Stop it this minute!" screamed Nora in her loudest voice. She tried to sound like Mommy.

"You heard what I said, and you are making me very angry."

Suddenly, even though she was the baby-sitter and it was time for Russell's nap, Nora couldn't

help herself. She began to bounce on the bed too.

Next they all got down on the floor and did somersaults, bumping into one another. They crawled under the bed, where it was dark and spooky. And finally they all felt tired, and they lay down on the big bed again. This time they fell asleep.

Nora opened her eyes first. There stood Mommy, with a haircut and earrings and lipstick, and Mrs. Michaels in her dress with her hair pinned up. They were both crying and laughing at the same time.

"It's my fault," said Mrs. Michaels. "I forgot to remind you that we were switching days this week."

"No, no," said Mommy, tears running down her cheeks. "It's all my fault. I should have remembered."

"I shouldn't have left Russell and run off."

"How terrible that I just went off leaving Nora and Teddy here all alone. . . ."

"How awful. . . ."

Nora sat up in the bed. "Mommy," she said, beaming. "It was wonderful. No one took me to school, so I stayed home and *I* was the baby-sitter."

Mommy hugged her and hugged her.

Then Nora said, "Mommy, it was fun. But tomorrow I will need a day off."

Daddy's Birthday

When Nora had her birthday, five girls from kindergarten came for a party. They brought presents, played pin-the-tail-on-the-donkey, ate cake and ice cream, and even after they went home Nora had worn her party dress. It had been a very special day.

When Teddy had his birthday, he had a party too. It was a smaller party, because Teddy was a smaller person. Russell had come upstairs after his nap. Another boy named Josh came too. Josh lived on a street nearby, and he often played with Teddy in the park. Teddy's friend Amy came also. Russell and Josh and Amy had all brought presents. And everyone had birthday cake and ice cream. Afterward they sat at the table, playing with big lumps of flour-and-salt dough that Mommy had made in the morning.

Today was Daddy's birthday. In the morning, before he went to work, Teddy and Nora had given him birthday kisses and hugs. But now that Daddy had left the house, the children began to worry about presents.

"Don't grown-ups get presents when they have a birthday?" asked Nora.

"Of course," said Mommy. "Daddy will get his present in the evening."

"What is he going to get?" asked Teddy.

Mommy went to the closet and took out a large package. "You can help me wrap this later," she offered.

"What is it?"

"Schubert string quartets," said Mommy, smiling proudly.

"I don't see any shoes," said Teddy. "Just records."

"And there aren't any strings," said Nora. "Besides Daddy likes ice cream better than shoobert. He told me last week when we bought ice-cream cones on the way home from the park."

"Schubert, not sherbert," said Mommy, laughing. "These are special phonograph records that Daddy's wanted for a long time."

"But what can *we* give him?" asked Teddy.

"The record album is a very big present," answered Mommy. "It will be from all of us, and you can both sign your names on the card."

"One present isn't enough," insisted Teddy. "What else can we give Daddy?"

"I'm going to bake a cake later, and you can both help mix the batter," suggested Mommy.

"Goody!" shouted Nora. "Can we lick the bowl too?"

"Of course."

"I want to give Daddy something special. Just from me alone," said Teddy.

"You don't have any money," pointed out Nora. It was true. Neither child had any money.

Teddy went to his room and looked around. Daddy liked books, and Teddy had lots of books. But Daddy had read them already when he read them aloud to Teddy and Nora each bedtime. Teddy wanted to give Daddy something new that he had never seen before.

Teddy opened the toy box. Maybe there was something inside that would be right. Inside there were little cars, teddy bears, a doctor kit, a toy telephone, broken crayons. Nothing that Daddy needed. Nothing that Daddy wanted.

Teddy kept thinking, but he could get no ideas. He helped Mommy and Nora fix the cake. Nora broke one egg into the bowl, and Teddy broke the other. Then Mommy took out the shell pieces, because they didn't go into the cake. They added sugar and flour and milk and put their fingers into

the bowl often, because it tasted so good. After the cake was finished, Mommy helped them to make chocolate frosting, which luckily was Daddy's favorite as well as theirs.

By then it was lunchtime. And after lunch, Teddy and Mommy took Nora to her kindergarten class.

"How many candles will Daddy have on his cake?" asked Nora.

"Oh, three or four," said Mommy.

"Four!" shrieked Teddy. "I had four. Three and one to grow on."

"Daddy's older than four," scoffed Nora. "He needs about twenty candles."

"It's different when you are older," explained Mommy.

"It isn't as much fun," said Nora.

"Presents make a birthday fun. Daddy needs more presents," said Teddy.

"Maybe I can make him something special at school," said Nora, as she waved good-bye to Mommy and Teddy and walked down the steps to her kindergarten class.

Back at home Teddy was restless. "Why don't you draw a picture for Daddy?" suggested his mother.

"No! I'm not good at drawing. Nora makes better pictures than me."

"Daddy likes your pictures," protested Mommy.

"I want to make him something that he never saw before. Something very special," said Teddy.

"What could it be?" wondered Mommy. "Could you make Daddy a block tower or a building?"

"Would he like that?" asked Teddy.

"It is something only you could make," explained Mommy. "No other tower would ever be exactly the same."

"But it will have to come down," said Teddy. "It wouldn't last."

"Birthdays don't last either," said Mommy. "Just happy memories. . . ."

Teddy went to the bedroom. He pulled the sack of blocks into the hallway.

"Mommy, can I build Daddy's birthday tower in your bedroom as part of the surprise?"

"All right," agreed Mommy, although the children's toys were generally not permitted in there.

Teddy began to work. He made the foundation of colored blocks and then began to build the tower. He worked slowly and cautiously, adding block by block with great concentration. In the end he used every block in his set. The tower was very grand, and he was proud of it. It was his special gift for Daddy.

When Nora came home from school, she admired the tower. She had made a finger painting for Daddy in her class.

The children waited eagerly for the afternoon to pass. At last they heard Daddy's key in the door. They ran to greet him with kisses.

"Daddy! I made you a birthday tower!" shouted Teddy, too excited to hold back the surprise.

"Great!" said Daddy. "I'll look at it right away." Daddy went into the bedroom to hang up his jacket. Teddy and Nora followed behind, so they saw what happened. Daddy went into the bedroom and banged into the tower. It swayed for an instant and then fell onto the floor with a crash. Even the bedroom rug couldn't muffle the sound,

and Mommy came running in from the kitchen.

"My tower!" screamed Teddy. "I made it for your birthday." He began to howl.

"Don't cry!" commanded Daddy. "It's my birthday, and I won't allow crying. Besides it was my tower, and I'm not crying."

"I can't help it!" sobbed Teddy.

Nora ran to get her finger painting. "Teddy. This can be from both of us," she said.

Daddy sat down on the floor. "Teddy, let's you and me build a new superduper tower together," he said. So they did. It was fantastic. Teddy admitted that it was even better than the first.

"And when we crash this one down to put the blocks away, it won't matter," said Daddy. "Because we know that next time we will make another tower even more wonderful."

Afterward they had dinner and birthday cake— with only one candle.

"To grow on!" said Nora.

And everyone listened to Schubert and ate ice cream.

String Beans

It was Sunday, and Grandma and Grandpa had come for a visit. Everyone sat around the dinner table smiling as Daddy sliced the roast beef and Mommy passed the mashed potatoes and gravy. There was also a large serving bowl filled with string beans.

"I don't want any beans," said Teddy, pouting and pushing his plate away.

"Teddy," said Mommy. "Eat your food."

"I like string beans," said Nora, proudly biting into one of her beans.

"Of course you do," said Daddy. "Everyone likes string beans."

"No!" said Teddy. "Not me!"

"Well," said Grandpa. "I can remember a time when I had to eat too many beans. It was a long time ago, when I was a little boy about your age.

"I lived in the country then. Next door to my house there was a woman and her son. You may have heard about him. His name was Jack."

"Jack? I don't know anyone named Jack," said Teddy.

"Well," said Grandpa. "He was a lazy, unpleasant fellow. I never liked him too much. In the winter he always threw snowballs at everyone. But let me tell you what happened one day. Jack's mother needed money to buy some food, so she told Jack to take their cow to town and sell it. Only instead of selling it, he traded it away to a man in exchange for a handful of colored beans."

"*That* Jack!" shouted Teddy and Nora. "Grandpa, did you really know *that* Jack who had the beanstalk?"

"I sure did," answered Grandpa. "I thought you might have heard about him. He got awfully famous for being so foolish. He brought those colored beans home, and his mother just threw them out the window and sent Jack upstairs to bed. Then she came over to our house, and we shared our supper with her. We even sent a sandwich back for that boy Jack. They don't tell about it in any of the stories.

"In the morning, when I was leaving for school, I saw an enormous thing growing outside of Jack's house."

"The beanstalk!" cried Teddy and Nora with delight.

"Yes, that's right," said Grandpa. "I knocked on Jack's door and asked if he wanted to walk to school with me. But that boy said he was going to stay home and climb to the top of his beanstalk."

"To the giant!" shouted Nora.

"Fee-fi-fo-fum!" called out Daddy, as he passed the meat platter.

"What happened next?" asked Teddy.

"Well," said Grandpa. "The teacher was furious with Jack. He was a bad student. He never paid attention in class or did his homework. And now he was playing hooky as well."

"Is that like playing hockey?" asked Nora.

"Hooky is when you stay home from school and you aren't sick," explained Mommy.

"Right," said Grandpa. "There we all were studying away and that naughty boy Jack was playing hooky. I was sure he would get into trouble. But when I came home from school that afternoon, there was Jack holding a hen that could lay golden eggs, which he had found at the top of the beanstalk. Everyone thought he was wonderful! When the teacher came to complain to Jack's mother, Jack gave her a golden egg.

"And the next day Jack stayed home from school again and climbed the beanstalk a second time, and he brought back—"

"A bag of gold!" shouted Teddy.

"Right!" said Grandpa. "And the next day he stayed home from school again. This time he got a golden harp, only this time the giant started to follow him down the beanstalk. So when he reached the bottom, he shouted to his mother to bring him an axe."

"And she did, and he chopped down the beanstalk," said Nora.

"Wrong!" said Grandpa. "All those books are wrong! Jack's mother wasn't home. She was out spending the gold pieces. But luckily I had just returned from school. I ran and got my axe, and I chopped the beanstalk down for him."

"Oh, Grandpa. That's wonderful!" breathed Nora.

"Did you see the giant fall?" asked Teddy.

"Of course," said Grandpa. "They may not write about me in the story, but I was there."

"Then what happened?" asked Nora.

"Well, we buried the giant. He made an enormous hole where he landed, and we filled it in with dirt. As for the beanstalk, it had so many beans on it that we picked for three weeks without stopping. Even Jack stopped being lazy and helped to pick. We had string beans for dinner every night for a month. And string-bean soup for lunch and even string-bean cereal for breakfast in the morning.

"That was a long, long time ago, but I still think of it whenever I have string beans for dinner," said Grandpa.

"Teddy, where are your beans?" asked Grandma.

"Did you throw them on the floor?" asked Nora.

Teddy looked down at his plate. He looked under the table. Then he smiled. "I guess I ate them," he said.

The Giant Party

Mrs. Wurmbrand sat drinking a cup of tea with Mommy. She told Mommy that she had gotten a letter that morning from her daughter in Cleveland. "She is coming to spend a week with me, and I am delighted," said Mrs. W. "Only. . . ."

"Only what?" asked Mommy.

"I know she wants me to return to Cleveland with her," said Mrs. Wurmbrand with a sigh. Her usually smiling face looked sad.

"Mrs. W! Will you move away from us?" Nora asked. She had been sipping her milk so quietly at the table that the two women had almost forgotten her presence.

"I don't know." Mrs. W. sighed again, then smiled sorrowfully. "I don't want to move. But I know that my daughter worries about me being so far away from her and all alone."

"You're not alone!" Nora cried, hugging Mrs. Wurmbrand. "You said we were like your family. You have us and all the other people in the building."

"I know. I only wish I could make my daughter understand what a wonderful big family I have here," the old woman said.

"When is she coming?" asked Mommy.

"The first of next month," Mrs. W. said.

"You must let me help you, and of course you will both come to dinner," said Mommy. "We will make a dinner party for her."

It was at that moment that Nora got her big idea.

When Mrs. W. left, Nora explained it to Mommy. "We must make a giant party for Mrs. W., so her daughter can see how special our building is. We have to invite everyone—two hundred people!"

"Nora! Use your head," said Mommy. "We can't fit twenty people in our apartment, let alone two hundred."

Teddy had the answer.

"We can have a party for two hundred people in the big front lobby."

"Teddy!" shrieked Nora. "You are so smart."

"Yes," said Teddy.

"We can't have a party in the lobby," said Mommy. "Whoever heard of such a thing? We would get in Henry's way. . . ."

"Mommy, we will invite Henry and everyone else. Everyone loves parties!"

So that is how it began.

Mommy spoke to Daddy. They both spoke to Mr. and Mrs. Michaels and Mr. and Mrs. Murphy and to several other neighbors as well. They rang doorbells and they collected some money and they invited everyone. Some people offered to prepare food. Their friend Anita suggested that she could decorate the lobby for the occasion. One neighbor worked for a supermarket, and he offered to donate three cases of soda.

Everyone was invited. Even grouchy old Mrs. Mind-Your-Own-Business was invited. She didn't say whether or not she would come. She did say it would probably make a mess in the front lobby. "Be sure that you clean up properly!" she scolded.

When Nora saw the dog owners in the elevator, she invited the dogs. Henry was skeptical. He had worked in this building for ten years and in another building before for twelve years, and he had never heard of such a thing.

"It sounds crazy," he kept saying.

Everyone knew about the party; everyone talked about the party; everyone prepared for the party. Except Mrs. W. She only knew that she was invited to dinner with her daughter on Friday evening, the third of May.

Nora and Teddy were very proud. They loved

their secret. Once they almost told Mrs. W. It would have been so much fun to tell her. But they didn't, because they knew the giant surprise party would be the most fun of all.

"Couldn't she have a heart attack from the shock?" worried Daddy.

"No. It will be a very low-key party," promised Mommy. "No lights off. No shouting." Besides, Dr. Greenberg, who lived on the ground floor, said that he was coming to the party.

To Nora it seemed as if the day would never arrive. It was as hard as waiting for her own birthday. She was curious to meet Mrs. Wurmbrand's daughter too.

To the children's amazement, the daughter closely resembled the mother. They had not expected the daughter to be another white-haired lady.

"She is sixty-three years old," Nora overheard her mother saying to Daddy the next day.

Any other time the dinner would have been an exciting affair. Tonight it dragged too slowly.

Nora and Teddy could scarcely eat. Luckily the grown-ups became so absorbed in conversation that no one seemed to notice.

When the main course was cleared from the table, it was Mommy's cue to say, "Mrs. W., I have a little surprise. We have all been invited to have dessert with Mr. and Mrs. Murphy in their apartment on the first floor. They wanted to meet your daughter too."

"What nice neighbors you have, Mama," said Miss Wurmbrand to her mother.

Nora poked Teddy, but neither of them said anything.

They all went into the elevator together. Teddy pressed the button marked *G* for ground floor.

Nora held her breath.

Daddy whistled his favorite melody from Schubert.

The elevator went down.

The door opened.

There was the lobby that Nora walked through almost every day of her life. It was completely transformed. Paper streamers and ribbons and balloons decorated it. Two enormous vases of flowers were on either side of the elevator door. A large table—actually several tables pushed together—stood holding plates of cookies and cakes. Another table held paper cups and bottles and bottles of soda.

But most exciting were all the neighbors. They stood along the walls in an orderly line, everyone wearing their party clothes.

Daddy counted and later reported more accurately that thirty-seven people and two dogs were in the lobby. Russell was there with his parents. Anita's boyfriend had come with his guitar, which he strummed softly. And, of course, Henry was standing there, right in front. Even Mrs. Mind-Your-Own-Business had decided it was her business to attend the party.

Mrs. Wurmbrand stood looking dumbfounded.

"What is this?" asked her daughter.

"It's a party!" squealed Nora. "A giant party for Mrs. W!"

Then everyone began to talk at once. They were

hugging and kissing and eating and drinking and singing and barking (from the dogs). There were a few chairs, so that the older people could sit down. But most people walked about talking and joking with one another.

"I just can't understand this," said Miss W. "Do you have parties like this often?"

"Actually we don't," admitted Nora's daddy. "But we did want to show you how much we care about your mother."

"Please, don't take her to Cleveland," begged Nora. "We need her. She is our extra grandmother."

"I know, she told me," said Miss Wurmbrand. "Could I be something too?"

"My daughter is thinking about moving to New York City, permanently." Mrs. W. smiled. "She said if I won't come to her, she will have to come to me."

"Why don't things like this get into the newspaper?" mused Mrs. W.'s daughter. "When I read about New York City back home, I worry all the time."

"There is a lot to worry about," said Mrs. Mind-Your-Own-Business, who had overheard the conversation.

"Don't worry so much!" said Mr. Murphy. "Relax. Enjoy life, like your mother does."

"Whose idea was this party?" asked Mrs. Wurmbrand, looking about.

Mrs. Murphy looked at Mrs. Michaels, who looked at Daddy, who looked at Mommy, who looked at Nora.

"It was Nora's idea," said Mommy proudly.

"Teddy helped," said Nora.

"Where is Teddy?" asked Mommy suddenly. They looked about the lobby and found him quickly. He was asleep under one of the tables. Daddy carried him upstairs to bed. But Nora was allowed to stay up till the very end of the giant party.

"Well," said Henry to Nora, when it was all over. "So you did it! You had your giant party after all."

"Yes," said Nora. "I knew I would."